*March 2025*

# Bella The Scientist Goes to Outer Space

By Silvana Spence & Isabella Spence

Illustrated by Darwin Marfil

*atmosphere press*

# Dedication

To my children, friends and family who always believed in me.
And every child who one day dreamed to become a scientist.
Go for it! You can do it!

Bella is an eight-year-old who loves math and science. Her favorite things are building different structures, playing video games, and conducting science experiments.

Vicky is a thirteen-year-old who loves nature,
reading, writing, and science.

Bella and Vicky are sisters,
and they both share a passion for scientific adventures.

One day, Bella asked, "I wonder what different types of scientists are out there, and if they all wear lab coats and goggles while doing their scientific experiments?"

"That's a great question, Bella," Vicky replied. "I wonder that, too.
Let's ask Cody!"

The girls turned to the iPad on the table.

"Cody, could you tell us what types of scientists there are?" asked Bella.

The iPad's screen lit up.

"Here is a list of the different types of scientists," Cody answered.

"Whoa! That is a long list!" Vicky said.

The girls scrolled through the long list of scientists
with wide eyes.

"So, which one should we start studying?" Vicky asked Bella.

"Well, I'd love to start with the Astronomer!" Bella replied.

"Astronomers investigate stars, planets and galaxies,"
Cody stated as pictures of the solar system and scientists
looking through telescopes appeared on the screen.

"That sounds like a great adventure!" Bella exclaimed.

Vicky nodded in agreement.

"Cody, take us to outer space!" Vicky and Bella shouted together.

"Okay, let's go!" Cody exclaimed as a flash of light shot from his screen.

When the light dimmed, the girls gasped.

Cody had teleported them onto the **VOIAGE 1** spaceship at **NASA**.

They couldn't believe their eyes!
The space shuttle was about to take off
for an outer space mission.

Bella and Vicky counted down, "5,4,3,2,1 BLAST OFF!"

"Wow!!" exclaimed the girls as they entered outer space.
Everywhere they looked they were surrounded by stars.

"Vicky," Cody said, "do you see that ball of fire faraway?"

"Yes! It's beautiful!" Vicky replied.

"Is that the Sun?" asked Bella.

"That's right, Bella! That's the Sun. Unlike the Earth, the Sun is not a planet. It's a star. It is an almost perfect sphere of super-hot gases whose gravity holds the solar system together," Cody told them.

"What's that small planet on the left?" Bella asked.

"That's Mercury! It takes 87.97 days for Mercury to orbit around the Sun. That means it has the shortest year of all the planets in the solar system," explained Cody.

"Oh, my gosh! That is a short year," Vicky said, shocked.

"Especially when compared to the Earth. It rotates around the Sun for 365 days, right Cody?" Bella checked.

"That is right!" Cody agreed.

"Bella, look at the next planet!" exclaimed Vicky.

Bella looked out the window with Vicky.

"Oh, I know the next one!" stated Bella. "It's Venus, the second planet from the Sun. It's the closest planet to Earth and one of the brightest objects we see in the sky."

"I know a few more fun facts about Venus," Cody added. "It is the hottest planet in our solar system, though not as hot as the Sun. Also, it has no moon."

"The next one is our planet, Earth," Cody pointed out.

"It's the third planet from the Sun, and the only place we know that's inhabited by living things," Vicky said. "I remember that from science class."

"It's also made up of four main layers," added Bella. "There's an inner core, surrounded by an outer core, then the mantle, and finally the crust. On top of that, the Earth has an ocean covering almost 70% of the planet's surface."

Bella smiled as she turned to Cody, "I did a school project on the Earth's layers last week."

"Great job, girls!" Cody congratulated them. "You are both exactly right!"

As the girl's traveled through space, they came upon another planet.

"Mars is the fourth planet from the Sun," Cody said as the girls looked out the window. "It's a dusty, cold, desert planet with a thin atmosphere. This planet has weather, seasons, canyons, polar ice caps, and extinct volcanoes."

"It's so red!" noted Vicky.

"Great observation," Cody said. "The surface of Mars is reddish-brown due to the rusting process of surface minerals."

"Another name for Mars is The Red Planet, right Cody?" Bella asked.

"That's right!"

"Whoa!" Vicky gasped. "What's that?"

The girls watched as the spaceship flew through a field of huge, floating rocks.

"This is the Asteroid Belt," said Bella. "It is the largest collection of asteroids in our solar system. Asteroids are rocky objects, smaller than planets, that orbit around the Sun. I learned about it in class, too!"

"Wow, I didn't know this existed!" Vicky said in awe.

"The Asteroid Belt orbits between Mars and the next planet, Jupiter, which you can see coming up now!" Cody said.

ASTEROID
BELT

As they approached the planet, Vicky's mouth fell open. "Whoa! It's enormous!"

"Jupiter is the fifth planet from the Sun," Cody said. "It is the largest planet in our solar system. Jupiter is known as a gas giant, which means it doesn't have a solid surface. Instead, the planet is made up of gases and liquids that are constantly swirling around."

"Because it's so big, it must take Jupiter a long time to fully rotate," Bella observed.

"Actually, Jupiter rotates extremely fast, so one day is only 10 Earth hours!" Cody corrected.

"What's that red swirling spot?" Vicky asked.

"That's known as the Great Red Spot. It's a storm that has been raging for hundreds of years," Cody stated. "It's one of Jupiter's most distinct characteristics."

"I know the next one!" Bella exclaimed. "It's Saturn, the sixth planet from the Sun."

"Correct," Cody confirmed. "It is the second-largest planet in our solar system. Like Jupiter, Saturn is also a gas giant made up of mostly hydrogen and helium."

"It has beautiful rings." Vicky started counting, "There are one... two... three... four... five... six... seven of them!"

"That's right," Cody said. "Those rings are made up of ice, dust, and rock. It is believed that some of these chunks are from asteroids, comets, and even shattered moons."

"Speaking of moons," Bella added, "Saturn has 82! Though only 53 have been confirmed and named."

"Uranus is the seventh planet from the Sun," Cody said as they neared the next planet. "It has 13 faint rings and 27 small moons."

"Its rings aren't as pretty as Saturn's," Vicky observed.

"I agree, but Uranus has a different characteristic that sets it apart," Bella informed her sister. "It is the only planet that spins on its side as it orbits the Sun."

"Right again, Bella," Cody praised. "Uranus is also known as an ice giant, rather than a gas giant, because it is made up of heavier gases and has an icy core. Methane is one of those gases, and that's why it has a blue color."

"Neptune, the eighth planet from the sun, is also known as an ice giant," Cody told the girls. "It is the fourth largest planet in the solar system."

"This planet is blue, just like Uranus," Vicky noted. "Does that mean its atmosphere contains methane, too?"

"Yes, it does!" Cody said.

"Neptune is also the last planet in our solar system," Bella stated.

"Wait, but what about that one?" Vicky asked, pointing to a small sphere in the distance.

"That's Pluto," Bella said. "It used to be considered a planet like all the others, but it was reclassified as a dwarf planet in 2006."

"Pluto is one of several dwarf planets at the end of our solar system," Cody added. "Together, with a variety of other icy objects, they make up the Kuiper Belt."

"It's even smaller than Earth's moon," Vicky noted.

PLUTO

"Wow," Bella said, "this trip has been—whoa, whoa! What was that?!"

The spaceship started shaking, tumbling the girls around.

"Why is the spaceship shaking so much?" yelled Vicky.

"I think an asteroid almost hit us! Is this normal for space adventures?" asked Bella.

"It wasn't an asteroid," Cody clarified. "Those were meteoroids! A meteoroid is created when a small piece breaks off an asteroid or a comet. When a meteoroid enters the Earth's atmosphere, it becomes a meteor as it flashes across the night sky and burns up. These are also called shooting stars."

The spaceship stopped shaking, and Bella and Vicky let out a sigh of relief.

"I didn't know being an astronomer could be so dangerous," Vicky said.

"Astronomers don't take trips into space," Bella replied. "Astronomers do all their work from Earth. Astronauts are the ones who work from spaceships."

"That's right," Cody said. "Astronomers research celestial bodies from Earth. They use telescopes, radars, computers and other special tools to share detailed information from outer space. The Hubble Space Telescope and the Spitzer Space Telescope are famous for sending important information to astronomers. They work together with astronauts to learn more about space and keep Earth safe."

"My favorite astronaut is Mae C. Jemison," Vicky stated. "She was the first black woman to travel into space when she served as a Mission Specialist aboard the Space Shuttle Endeavour. But I don't think I know any famous astronomers."

"I do," Bella chipped in. "Dr. Neil deGrasse Tyson fell in love with astronomy when he was our age. When he grew up, he earned his master's degree in astronomy, and then he earned his PhD in astrophysics, which is the combination of studying astronomy and physics!"

"This trip has been amazing! I'd love to go on a second outer space adventure, but for now I think I'm ready to return to Earth," said Vicky.

"I agree," Bella said. "I can't wait to share all the wonderful things that we learned."

"Cody, please take us back!" the girls requested.

"Secure your seat belts and let's go!" Cody replied.

They zoomed through the solar system as planets blurred past, and before they knew it, Vicky, Bella and Cody were back at their home. They arrived just as their mom walked into the room.

"Girls! Where were you?" their mom asked. "I've been looking for you everywhere."

Vicky and Bella smiled at each other and said together, "Do you really want to know?"

Hi friends!

Thank you for going on an outer space adventure with us today. If you want to continue your space adventure at home, we have a cool experiment for you. We are going to teach you how to make rocket vinegar. Make sure to do this experiment outside with an adult.

# Rocket Vinegar Experiment

## Materials
1. 1 empty, clean 8-ounce water bottle
2. ½ cup of vinegar
3. 2 tablespoons of baking soda
4. 1 cork
5. 1 funnel

## Instructions
Step 1: Using a funnel, pour ½ cup of vinegar into a clean and empty 8-ounce water bottle.
Step 2: Rinse and dry the funnel.
Step 3: Using the funnel, pour 2 tablespoons of baking soda into the water bottle.
Step 3: Cover the open top of the water bottle with a cork. Gently turn the bottle upside-down while holding the cork tight, to keep it from spilling.
Step 4: Quickly turn the bottle upright, set it down, and step back to watch the rocket take flight.

# Rocket Vinegar Experiment

## Tips and Tricks

1. If you want a bigger rocket, increase the amount of vinegar and baking soda accordingly. This might mean you'll need a bigger bottle, too!

2. The bigger the rocket, the bigger the mess, so be sure to prepare your space.

3. Remember to step away from the rocket as soon as the chemical reaction starts!

## Explanation

When baking soda, which is a base, mixes with the vinegar, which is an acid, it causes a chemical reaction that creates carbon dioxide. As the carbon dioxide gas fills the inside the bottle, the built-up pressure rushes towards the opening, launching the cork into the air

# The Scientific Method

EXPERIMENT TITLE: ROCKET VINEGAR

OBSERVATION:

PROCEDURE:

HYPOTHESIS:

ANALYSIS:

METHOD:

CONCLUSION:

Name: _____

Date: _____

Class: _____

Teacher: _____

# GREAT JOB!

You learned a lot about the solar system today!

What were your favorite facts about the planets? Use the next few pages to write down some of the things you learned.

Then, create your own planet! What would you name it? What would it look like? How many moons would it have? Record your answers on the Planet Research sheet.

# SOLAR SYSTEM

What I learned about the Solar System:

| FACT 1 |
| --- |
|  |

| FACT 2 |
| --- |
|  |

## FACT 3

# PLANET RESEARCH

Name:                                          Date:

My Planet:

**Appearance:**

**Temperature:**

**Distance from the Sun:**

**Number of Moons:**

**Interesting Facts:**

# About the Author

Silvana is an educator in Florida, a graduate of FIU School of Education with a Bachelor's in Early Childhood Education and a Master's degree in Curriculum and instruction. Silvana lives in Jacksonville, FL with her husband and two daughters Isabella co-author, and Victoria who is portrayed as the character in this book. Her love for education and children lead her to write engaging stories, where children are represented and to motivate them to read and love science.

Isabella Spence always loved STEAM. Her scientific interests lead her mom to write this book. She has a YouTube channel where she shares science experiments and her new hobby for making Roblox videos.

# About Atmosphere Press

Atmosphere Press is an independent, full-service publisher for excellent books in all genres and for all audiences. Learn more about what we do at atmospherepress.com.

We encourage you to check out some of Atmosphere's latest releases, which are available at Amazon.com and via order from your local bookstore:

*Gloppy*, by Janice Laakko
*Wildly Perfect*, by Brooke McMahan
*How Grizzly Found Gratitude*, by Dennis Mathew
*Do Lions Cry?*, by Erina White
*Sadie and Charley Finding Their Way*, by Bonnie Griesemer
*Silly Sam and the Invisible Jinni,* by Shayla Emran Bajalia
*Feeling My Feelings*, by Shilpi Mahajan
*Zombie Mombie Saves the Day*, by Kelly Lucero
*The Fable King*, by Sarah Philpot
*Blue Goggles for Lizzy*, by Amanda Cumbey
*Neville and the Adventure to Cricket Creek*, by Juliana Houston
*Peculiar Pets: A Collection of Exotic and Quixotic Animal Poems*, by Kerry Cramer
*Carlito the Bat Learns to Trick-or-Treat*, by Michele Lizet Flores
*Zoo Dance Party*, by Joshua Mutters
*Beau Wants to Know*, a picture book by Brian Sullivan
*The King's Drapes*, a picture book by Jocelyn Tambascio
*You are the Moon*, a picture book by Shana Rachel Diot
*Onionhead*, a picture book by Gary Ziskovsky
*Odo and the Stranger*, a picture book by Mark Johnson
*Jack and the Lean Stalk*, a picture book by Raven Howell
*Brave Little Donkey*, a picture book by Rachel L. Pieper
*Buried Treasure: A Cool Kids Adventure*, a picture book by Anne Krebbs
*Young Yogi and the Mind Monsters*, an illustrated retelling of Patanjali by Sonja Radvila
*The Magpie and the Turtle*, a picture book by Timothy Yeahquo

www.ingramcontent.com/pod-product-compliance
Lightning Source LLC
Chambersburg PA
CBHW060039280125
20961CB00024B/1414